Valentine F...

By April Jones Prince
Illustrated by Elisabeth Schlossberg

To DRP . . . my forever Valentine.

ISBN-13: 978-0-439-79999-7
ISBN-10: 0-439-79999-6

10 9 8 7 6 5 4 3 2   07 08 09 10 11 12

Printed in the U.S.A.
First printing, January 2007

Cartwheel
·B·O·O·K·S·®

SCHOLASTIC INC.
New York Toronto London Auckland Sydney
Mexico City New Delhi Hong Kong Buenos Aires

Dog draws.

Cat cuts.

Pig pastes.

Snail shuts.

Friends make valentines!

Penguin pours.

Seal sifts.

Stork stirs.

Lion lifts.

Friends bake valentines!

Though half the fun

is in preparing...

Valentine's Day
is made for sharing!